show off

edited by Joe Bunting

The Write Practice
2813 Shades Valley Lane,
Gainesville, GA 30501

Copyright © 2012 by The Write Practice

Paperback ISBN 978-0-9884497

Cover by Zak Erving

thewritepractice.com

Contents

JOE BUNTING

Editor's Note: Secrets

I spoke with a writer recently who confessed, "To be known or not known seems to be the enduring question. I've always wanted both." It reminded me of an essay in Glimmer Train from a West Virginian writer named Natalie Sypolt. She was feeling insecure about writing about her poor, "redneck" family. "There wasn't an epiphany," she said, "but a gradual understanding that to really be a writer, I had to get beyond my fear and write the truth."

Honestly, sometimes it's easier to write spectacular stories, full of plot twists and car chases, populated by fascinating heroes and despicable villains, than it is to write the truth. In other words, you can write formulaic stories based on the television mystery model—where the clever, stubborn detective surmounts all odds and catches his man—more easily than you can write a good story about home, about family, about the normal, everyday mysteries of life. As far as I know, the ten stories in this collection are fictional, but they are also all true.

Good stories are confessional booths: We, the readers, go in as priests to absolve (or not) the sins of others. The best stories, though, the ones that connect with the deep places in us, invite us to kneel on that hard wood and stare at the screen and say, yes, yes, it was me, I did it, how did you know?

These ten stories are the confessions we hold in the secret places of our souls. These are the stories we rarely show off.

—Joe Bunting
thewritepractice.com

MARLA CANTRELL

Miss Maize County's Public Disgrace

It all started because Mama got caught standing buck-naked in the picture window of her living room. The sheriff come out and talked to me about it. Her house set across from Harmony Baptist and the Sunday morning crowd had gotten an up-close-and-personal look at her. Even hell-fire-and-brim-stone can't compete with a naked lady standing atop a divan, kind of spread eagled and pressed up against a plate glass window.

After the sheriff's visit, I brought Mama to my house. She had days when she was fine, and then there were days when she was as lost as a ball in tall grass. She'd wander. She'd forget who I was. When I found her wading with the cows in the neighbor's pond, I called on Doc Patton, who put his hand on my shoulder and told me to check her into the nursing home. Which I did.

The story should have ended there, with Mama in the rest home, me alone in my trailer, and Brother Debo at the pulpit, preaching to the fully clothed. But then Brother Debo come by. I opened my door and there he was, dressed like he was fixing to preach a funeral. "Miss Huggins," he said. "I don't believe we've met. I'm Ransom Debo. I was wondering if we might have a little talk." Once inside, I swept the magazines off the divan and motioned for him to sit.

"Florene," I said. "My name's Florene." I sat facing him.

"What can I help you with?" I asked. He took my hand.

"Doctor Patton mentioned you had to put your mother away. I'm so sorry. I didn't know her well, but she did visit me at the church a time or two. Lovely woman."

"Wait a minute, preacher," I said. "Don't go acting like you cared about Mama. If that was the case, you wouldn't have called the law on her like you done."

He let loose of my hand and fiddled with his tie tack. It was a tiny gold bible with a ruby where the "O" in holy should have been. I looked right at him. He wasn't much older than me. Maybe thirty-two or thirty-three. And handsome. Even in that preacher get-up, he was handsome.

"Let's start over Miss Hugg…, I mean Florene. I'm truly concerned about your mother." He cleared his throat. "However, there is another reason I'm here."

"Big surprise," I said.

He kept going. "Your mother's house sits across

from the sanctuary, and our congregation needs the space. If we had your mother's house, we could move the adult Sunday school classes there."

I remember looking in his eyes. They were green with gray rims. Kind of like cat eyes.

"Well," I said. "I ain't giving Mama's property away."

Brother Debo smiled. One of his front teeth was chipped. "I find prayer helpful when I have an important decision to make," he said.

"Pray all you want," I said. "I'll be figuring out what Mama's house is worth."

Brother Debo started coming by once a week. He'd show up and ask if I'd decided anything, and I'd stand at the door, my arms folded, and tell him I was still debating. "No rush," he'd say, "just wondering." And then he'd walk back down my steps, his hands in his pocket, and every time he'd be whistling.

The fourth time he showed up, I told him the same thing, but this time I asked him in. It was something about the way he looked that day, like he needed company as much as I did, that made me do it.

It wasn't long before he stopped talking like a preacher. He started sounding kind of regular, like somebody you'd meet at the Piggly Wiggly on coupon night. After we'd worn out the subject of the

Cardinal's bad season and the Cowboy's good one, he asked me this.

"You ever been married, Florene?"

I looked past Brother Debo, to the window above the sink. "It's ain't something I talk about too much," I finally said, "but yeah, I been married. I was seventeen. I'd just been crowned Miss Maizie County for the third time. Ain't nobody beat my record, not in all these years.

"My husband was one of the judges. We didn't date until after I was crowned, I want you to know, so I earned my title fair and square.

"It ain't a remarkable story. He drank beer like it was oxygen and he was scared to death of a good day's work." I shook my head. "So, I left him and got my old name back."

Brother Debo took my hand for the second time since I'd met him.

"You know, Florene, I don't think divorce is so bad. If God can forgive lying and stealing, I don't see why he can't allow for a few failed nuptials."

He opened up to me then. Started talking about his shut-in wife, how she was practically bed-ridden with some mysterious muscle disorder. He mentioned how they weren't able to have relations. Had a way of telling it, made you think he was a saint for staying with her.

I started watching the road for his car, hoping he'd come by. Which he did, late one Friday night. He showed up on my steps, his Lincoln nowhere in sight. He followed me inside, circling his arms around me when I turned to him, and leaning me up against the paneling.

"It's wrong, I know it's wrong, but you're all I think about," he said.

I swear I almost called him Brother Debo, but I knew that two people about to do what we were would not be encouraged by religious titles.

I called him Ransom for the first time.

He kissed me, and I sagged against him.

"Are you sure you want to do this?" he asked.

"I could show you Grandma Cant's quilt," I said, and felt my face go red. "It ain't much but I could show you." I pointed down the hall. "It's on my bed.

"See," I said, when we got to my room, "it ain't much to look at."

"It's beautiful," he said, looking at me instead of the quilt. We sat down on my bed then, my three Miss Maizie County banners hanging on the wall above me, and I realized I was about to become a great sinner.

Damned if I didn't fall in love. We talked on the phone every day, and we made love every chance we got, and we didn't tell a soul.

I sold Mama's house, for too little money, on a Wednesday morning. The deacons shook my hand, and I walked out into the October sun, clutching a skinny cashier's check.

I called Ransom, and he didn't pick up. I called again, and he told me his secretary had seen my number come up too many times on his phone bill, in the early morning hours and late at night, and she was talking.

It must've been true. I was getting snubbed everywhere I went. On Saturday, Ransom's wife came to my house, leaning on a cane, and yelled at me, saying I'd seduced her husband same as Delilah troubled Sampson. I have one thing to say about that. For a shut-in, she sure had a good set of lungs.

I called Ransom when she left, but his number had been disconnected. I drove by the church. The sign announcing Sunday's sermon read: Genesis - It Was The Woman Who Sinned.

I knew then that Ransom had turned on me, and I felt something die inside. I bought a bottle of Wild Turkey and went down to the river.

The next morning, the sun spilled like heartbreak across Harmony Baptist. I could hear the choir from my spot inside

Mama's house, which hadn't been touched since the day she left. Ransom's sermon was long and loud, and it was noon before the invitation finally began.

I climbed onto the divan, my legs still shaky from the drinking. I pushed back the dusty curtains. The sun felt warm on my naked breasts.

I leaned against the window, listening as the last threads of "Rescue the Perishing" faded and then died, and ached for those church doors to open.

PATRICIA HUNTER

The Worst Christmas Ever

When Daddy grabbed the miniature Christmas tree off the table where I'd placed it by his wheelchair and crushed it with both hands, I was stunned.

The little tree had been the centerpiece on my parents' kitchen table for years. Crafted from dozens of tiny green and gold foil-wrapped boxes glued to an eighteen-inch Styrofoam cone, I couldn't remember a Christmas where it didn't stand on the kitchen table while Daddy worked his crossword puzzles. I'd hoped it would bring him a little joy and brighten his room in the nursing home. That he would destroy it was beyond my imagination, but then nothing about the day had unfolded as I'd expected.

Earlier, my eight-year-old daughter, Emily, and I stopped by Mother's room to leave the boxes of Christmas decorations. We'd known for years that Daddy had Alzheimer's, but Mother's rapidly declining health remained a mystery. She was sitting in a wheelchair with her untouched lunch tray on the table before her, obviously needing more help than the staff had provided. I removed the cover from the dinner plate, spread a paper napkin across her lap and seasoned the food so she could eat. "I'll be back after we check on Daddy," I assured her.

We found Daddy asleep, slumped to one side of his wheelchair in the hall outside his room. He was a mess. In desperate need of a haircut and shave, his rumpled clothes hung loosely on his tall, bony frame. Both arms were covered with bruises and a bandage was wrapped around his right forearm. He'd bitten into one of his medications and the reddish-brown remains mixed with drool and ran down the creases of his chin.

Waking him gently, I wheeled him back to his room, washed his face and showed him the bag of Christmas decorations we brought to decorate his side of the room. I removed the decorations from the bag and placed them on Daddy's bed. His bed, a bedside table, a small closet of drab, baggy clothes, and his wheelchair were all he had to show for the years he had worked—long past retirement age—to provide for his family.

I'd never known Daddy to be anything but gentle except for the time he punched Mother's roommate when she wouldn't let him through the door to see his wife. It was totally out of character for him to destroy the Christmas tree I'd put on the table next to him.

"Daddy! Why did you do that?" I cried, prying his fingers off the now ruined centerpiece, but he only groaned and stared over my shoulder.

I called for the nurses. Though they didn't want

to, I convinced them to put Daddy back in bed. "Maybe he just needs to rest," I told them as they removed his shoes and tucked the covers around his frail, lanky frame.

There was a hint of embarrassment in Mother's smile when I walked back into her room—like a little girl caught skipping through mud puddles, she knew she'd made a mess. Tomato sauce was smeared all around her lips and down her chin from the food she had managed to get to her mouth. The rest of her lasagna and green beans were either in her lap or on the floor.

I chuckled, trying to pretend nothing was wrong. I'd never seen my mother like this.

"How was your father?" she asked when I returned from the bathroom with warm water and a washcloth to clean her face. On most days, someone from the rehab center would take Mother to Daddy's room, or bring Daddy to her. Today would not be one of those days.

"I don't think he's feeling well today." I told her, praying she couldn't see the tears that threatened to spill or detect the lump in my throat.

We stayed with Mother as long as we could. Emily held her grandmother's hand and told her what she was learning in school and what she wanted for Christmas. With tinsel garland, we framed the bulletin board on the wall by her bed and placed other decorations around her side of the room. After reading her Christmas cards and tacking them to the newly decorated bulletin board, we kissed my mother goodbye.

It was the worst Christmas ever. Without waking up again, Daddy died two days after we left him that day, and Mother forgot how to brush her teeth. She forgot Daddy died, how to feed herself, or that we had moved her out of the rehab center two days before Christmas and into our home. On Christmas Eve, when it was time to leave for church, my family left without me. Mother could not be left alone. It was the first time in twenty years I was not at church with my family on Christmas Eve.

I recently asked Emily if she remembers visiting Daddy that day. She does not. Is it because she had only known Daddy with dementia? I wondered. That last Christmas with Daddy is one I will never forget.

Before we left that day, I crept back into Daddy's room, relieved to see him soundly asleep. I leaned over the bed rail, kissed his forehead and whispered, "I love you, Daddy." Grabbing the bag with the crushed Christmas tree, I left without disturbing him.

NANCY VANDRE

A Place to Call Home

My name is Anna and I am from Filer, Idaho, where the men fight over water rights and the women over first place ribbons for peach pie. I lived with my four sisters in the attic of my parent's barn-red farmhouse with purple and orange shag carpet. When I was fifteen, I would sneak out my window to meet Brett. Brett sang me songs on his guitar and shared his dreams about becoming the next John Lennon. Two years later, on the night Brett left, he gave me a pale green sapphire ring with delicate flanking diamonds. A ring which—two years after that—my mother made me throw in the trash because she (who'd married a man who'd given her a twenty year-old daughter and a nineteen year-old marriage certificate) had found the man I would marry.

I married in September 1980 and in the winter moved to Rexburg, ID, where the frozen fog glued my nostrils together. John Lennon was murdered that year. We lived in a 300 square-foot basement apartment with empty slots where kitchen drawers should have been and a floor that would scrunch underfoot from little black worms that oozed under the front door when it rained. I had an Associate's Degree in General Studies while He was perpetually undeclared: pre-med, radiology, tech school, a life-experience degree from an Idaho community college. My savings—from selling Cutco Knives—and wages—from working at Cascade Building Materials for a cigar-smoking boss who exhaled workforce wisdom like the Caterpillar from Alice in Wonderland—paid His tuition.

We had a hole in our bathroom door; every place we lived had a hole in that door. Shouting started it: the blame thrown my way for the job He could not keep, the child not growing in my womb. It inevitably ended with His fist and a termination of our lease.

From Rexburg we moved to the Bench near the Nevada border, just 40 miles south of Twin Falls, into a single-wide propane-powered trailer with a cat. I named him Mr. Lennon for his chipped tooth and black circles like glasses around his eyes. Mr. Lennon became ill and we had no Cutco savings to pay for the vet, so He took Mr. Lennon out back and forced his head into the water trough, keeping it there until Mr. Lennon was dead. We were living in that trailer with a cat grave to the west when my mother gave me a three-foot-nine-inch-dark-brown-Wurlitzer spinet with seventy-three keys. I played and played and played. We continued to try on our own for a baby until January 1985. Test results: not my fault. We visited the Utah Center for Reproductive Medicine where attractive, "fully tested," first year med-students donated their sperm for extra cash. I picked an anonymous father for my child. And when I went in for my intrauterine insemination, He did not come. Two weeks later, He sold my Wurlitzer for His version of a paycheck and we moved.

We moved into the top unit of a four-plex in Roy, Utah, adjacent to Hill Air Force Base. The front yard had a cherry tree with voluminous pink blossoms that trembled when He slammed the door and when the F-16 Fighting Falcons flew overhead. That summer, the sun scorched, and I mowed the lawn of the landlord's other properties to save money on rent while He worked at Radio Shack, and we saved enough to buy our first microwave for $600. Tommy came three weeks early on a hot sticky October evening after fourteen hours of labor and an emergency C-section. Tommy was fragile: five pounds, six ounces, nineteen inches long with jaundice. My mother came for a week and I took Percocet for two. Inventory revealed two Radio Shack VCRs and a TV missing: another job, another door, another lease.

This time we moved back to Filer. Back where I started, except for a pale green sapphire and the fact that John Lennon was dead. He worked for Dairygold Dairy and we lived in a small yellow house, at the edge of a cornfield behind my parent's barn. It had straw bales stacked against the outside walls for insulation and the shower was on the porch where icicles formed on the shower head and crystals on the walls. As the weather warmed, the petunias overtook the backside of the house and Tommy would load his dump truck with the fallen petals and surrounding dirt. When my parents came over for dinner, my father grunted for more spaghetti and my mother did not ask about my long sleeves in the summer. Just after Tommy's second birthday I had a baby girl by the same anonymous, attractive med student. I named her Grace, and then a Dairygold Dairy demotion moved us north.

We moved North, to Boise, to a sapphire-blue, split-entry house that sat on a cul-de-sac which flooded when it rained. We were homeowners and as such, I purchased a Rock-hide-a-key and hid a spare inside. Next door lived Bohemian flower children who taught me how to grow sunflowers that towered over the fence and that the shrubs I had trimmed were actually lilac bushes. The basement was cold but carpeted; it was where I did my projects. I sewed an oversized Bugs Bunny for Tommy and a Babs Bunny for Grace, Christmas stockings for the holidays, and a multi-color-faux-fur-patch bedspread for our queen-size waterbed. Grace took her naps on that bedspread while I found ways to hide my right eye with my bangs. Tommy liked to watch Star Wars and pretend his squirt gun was a Blaster. Once, Tommy heard the battle ensuing and came to the rescue only to end up a fallen solider in a crumpled heap against the bedroom wall. It was time to move again, but this time without Him. Without him to teach my son that violence was a language. Without him to convince my son that children were merely tax deductions. Without him to show my son that compassion was a frailty. Without him.

I went back to school at Boise State University and took my children with me. Grace started pre-school where she had nap-time and a tire-swing, and Tommy came with me to Cost and Managerial Accounting 403. Fall came with labeled backpacks and school lunches—Tommy was in charge of the key and the after-school snack. He taught Grace to tie her shoes and write her name on the chalkboard in our home. Our home was a two-bedroom end-unit University Heights student apartment with red-brick walls and a mini-fridge. Tommy and Grace shared one room with bunk beds, Barbies, and Power Rangers, while I, for the first time in my life, had a room of my own. On May 21, 1993, I hung a poster of John Lennon above my single pillowed full-size bed and watched the moon pass between me and the sun.

DOMINIC LAING

Ice, Custard, Happiness, Amen

House faces West, so early-day Sun climbs up back, and late-day Sun tumbles down front.

No one stoop-sits in cold months. Hands buried deep, hoodies and mittens pulled tight; Monks passing between prayers.

But sun re-shines and Vibrance spreads anew. Roy G. Biv comes out of retirement and clear-cool-blue rends Winter's tabernacle veil as far as Eye can see.

Eyes see further when Sun re-shines and Wind kicks out the bullshit. Blue be clear and cool, and brick be Red.

My eyes record Sun and Wind, Blue and Red.

Long morning. Slow. Funeral tomorrow.

II

Banshee Block. Where I live.

Young bulls rolling up, popping on two wheels like they hot shit. Four wheels, look like tanks, like they oughta be off-roading through Fairmount. In the desert, somewhere.

Not here, though.

They rev their motors, each one-by-one. They blow by each block in the hood, scaring all the old folks, making all the kids think the Banshees are the baddest. They don't care about the neighborhood. Each one with a mask or a hood, each one making sure my peace and quiet don't last long.

My head never settles, never rests.

To them, I bet they sound like Kings of the Jungle.

Don't sound like no lion to me. Don't sound like no cub neither. Sounds like a Jackal or a Hyena, like some punk in puberty. All squeals and squeaks. Ain't no roar to be found from any of 'em.

Hyenas, one and all.

III

Sitting at the service. Everyone looks smaller in coffins. No one looks like they did when they lived. I have a picture of her in my pocket. That's how I'm going to remember.

"She looks great."

"She looks nice, man."

"She's beautiful."

Dead, what she is.

We asked a friend to sing. Before he sang, he spoke.

"There was a woman," he said. "Sick for years; vomiting, bleeding. All these men trying to heal her, but she doesn't get well. Then she hears Jesus is coming to town. And she fights the crowd because she believes if she can just touch him, she'll be healed."

He looks at my family, and smiles.

"So Sam Cooke and the Soul Stirrers hear about this woman, and they go into the studio to write a song about her. Now, before I start, you have to know it's a hand-clapping song, so I'm gonna need your help.

And it goes something like this...

OHHHHHHHHHHHHHHH
There was a woman, in the Bible days,
she had been sick, sick so very long
but she heard about Jesus was passing by
so she joined the gathering throng
And while she was pushing her way through
Someone asked her 'what are you trying to do?'
She said 'if I could just touch the hem of his garment,
I know I'll be made whole...'

Later, the preacher preaches.

"She's been changed. She's not in a better place. No sir. She's not in a better place. That's how lies get spread, and we're not gonna spread lies. She's not in a better place. She's in the best place. The best place.

And you couldn't convince her to come back here, not for one second.

"She is now changed. From the temporal, to the eternal. From the corruptible to the incorruptible. From the decrepit to the intrepid; lost to found. Glory to God! Glory to God!

"Make sure," the preacher says, "make sure the love in this room doesn't stay here. Make sure you carry it out with you. Make sure it resounds."

I don't have any idea how there's love in this room. I don't feel love. I still feel loss. And pain.

The preacher's right, though. She can't get sick anymore, she can't break any bones, and she'll never have to see any more doctors.

And she's unreachable by phone. She has no permanent address, and I'll never be able to visit her on a Saturday again. I'll never be surprised by the presence of freshly-made dinner.

Never an unannounced visit. All visits from now until I die will be announced and planned. I'll always be going to visit on purpose and it'll always be to pay respects.

IV

First day of spring. Clear cool blue. Roy G. Biv out doing his thing. Looking fresh.

First day of spring means free Water-Ice at Rita's.

I get the Mango flavor; doesn't leave your mouth red like some damn lipstick. Sweet.

One-thirty; before school lets out, line's still long though. You gonna wait, but you always gonna wait for free Water Ice, and it's worth it.

I glance up at the sign. Under the name it reads, "Ice, Custard, Happiness."

All's I'm thinking about is how much I wish she were here, and how much I wish those Banshees would never come ripping down my block, how much I wish for peace and quiet...

...and how much I wish I could call her and hear her voice.

Two old ladies behind me.

"Whatchu doing tomorrow?"

"Some of the grandkids are coming over."

"Yeah?"

"Yeah. Gonna make cookies."

"Alright."

"Easter's in two weeks."

"Really?"

"MmmHmm."

"Shame; Jesus is gonna miss His free Water Ice."

First day of Spring. Me and the Garment. Make me whole.

KRISTI BOYCE

The Ride

We were heading home. A haze of dust trailed his Chevy as it rumbled down the dirt road. I looked at the two empty feeding buckets sitting at my feet and said, "Man, those horses sure do love oats, don't they?" He smiled back at me.

"Yep, they sure do."

I glanced in the rearview mirror—the horses' necks were craned to the ground, grazing. Tails swishing in the air, sweat-stained backs now free of saddles and cinches. We turned a corner and they disappeared. I didn't know it then, but it was one of our last rides together. Had I known, would home have beckoned so winsomely? Home, with its promise of cool water and clean hands. I cherished the ride, yes, but it felt so good to slide those musty riding gloves off my fingers—to run my hands under flowing water and scrub the sweat off my brow and the dirt from my palms. I loved him for his white hair and long silences and the peace I felt when I rode next to him. But I loved home, with its coolness and cleanness, too. If only I didn't have to say goodbye to one to have the other.

Earlier that morning, the reins jingled softly in my hands as we rode along a split-rail fence. A velvet breeze rustled the meadow. Prairie grass rose and fell, rose and fell as eight hooves rose and fell, rose and fell. We would talk occasionally, but never for very long. Cowboys don't talk much, but that wasn't the reason why. I didn't know the reason why.

A forest laid at the edge of the meadow, a cocoon of life and stillness. Thousands of delicate aspen leaves blocked the heat of the summer solstice, casting a tapestry of speckled shadows in every direction. Tall grass brushed against my stirrups with a ssshhhhh.

Why aren't we talking? I wondered. I was bursting with questions for him, about him. Questions about horses, the wars, atomic bombs, his childhood, his wife, his daughter (my mother). It was the longest day of the year and I had him to myself. Even so, I fidgeted in my saddle, worried that time would run out on my questions.

Didn't he know what a mystery he was? I had strewn together pieces from stories here, pictures there, a medal on the wall. But I was impatient. It was the summer I turned fourteen and I desperately wanted to learn not only about him, but about myself. His blood was my blood—there were answers there. But he was not the type of man you pushed for answers.

He was quiet and majestic, with a countenance both hard and soft. Warm grey eyes tempered the weathered lines running up, down, sideways on his face. I always sensed his mind was burdened with memories of war. Of questioning, maybe? Of where was God in the Second World War? In Korea? But the mountains live and breathe of God. And horses don't care who you are, or what you did, or why things are the way they are or why you don't talk more.

"Look," he said, pointing to the branches above.

Two dark eyes followed our movements. An owl. I held my breath instinctively as we trespassed through its little world. That simple, beautiful world that feels so natural and yet so foreign at times. The forest was a cathedral.

Maybe that was the reason why we weren't talking.

§

I bet his horses remember him. I bet they miss seeing him drive up to the pasture in his old Chevy with two big buckets of oats in the back.

But that's okay. Because he's home now. And he's scrubbed the sweat off his brow and the dirt from his palms and is relishing the memory of a good, good ride.

§

Ten years have passed. It was everything to me then; it is everything to me now. So beautiful a memory that I sometimes wonder whether it really happened.

The meadow, the forest, the owl: they were before it all. Before he got sick. Before he got better. Before he got sick again. Before he made one final trip to Big Thompson Canyon and this rugged cowboy— this atomic scientist, this Marine, this man who was so strong and yet so meek—stood in the pasture and wept softly as he said goodbye to his horses.

MORGAN O'CONNOR

Relay

The day before Christmas and we were getting drunk at the 19th Hole, our local golf course bar, which was almost buried in snow. There was a roaring fire and Wally, the barman and an old kindergarten classmate, brought over four long Jameson's on ice.

"Welcome home boys. This round is on the Inn," said Wally.

We raised our glasses and toasted Wally, The Maplewood Golf Course and Inn, the town, the lake, snow, summer, leaving town, our school and especially our tenth grade math teacher, Miss Miotto, who had the body of a cello. All home for the holidays, our talk ranged from work to sports to wives to kids and usually ended up back in town, revolving around some trivial memory.

"You guys hear about Zubic?" asked Sid, a dentist in San Francisco.

"Yeah, he went out to the Rockies and became a ski instructor or park ranger or something."

"He died in March. Burned to death in a shack."

"No."

"No."

"No. Really?"

"Guess he was doing some early spring ice fishing, the wood stove caught fire and incinerated him, the shack and three Huskies. I can't believe you guys didn't hear anything."

"An accident?"

"So they say."

"Was he wasted?"

"He was ice fishing. Probably."

"Why didn't anyone email me?" I asked.

We stared at the fire, ordered another pitcher.

"Remember that track-meet where Zubic broke his arm?" said Brent, a hedge-fund manager in Toronto.

"Yeah."

"Yeah. High-jump, right? He jumped the mat," said Sid.

"I don't remember that," I said.

"Sure you do. You were there. I remember because we bribed you to drop the baton in the 400m relay," said Godfry, now a pastry instructor at LeCordonBleu Chef school in Key West.

"I remember it like it was yesterday."

"I remember dropping the baton," I admitted, "but it was an accident. It banged my knee and slipped out of my hand. We were disqualified. Sorry, but there was no bribe. No money changed hands."

"Bull."

"No way."

"I can't believe you don't remember. It changed my opinion of you completely," said Harlen, a pilot for FedEx, who moved cities so quickly we stopped asking.

"Why would you guys bribe me? Why would my own teammates bribe me to drop our own baton?" I asked.

"No one wanted to run. It was the last event of the day. We were dead."

"Yeah, it was a scorcher. I had a sunburn on the back of my legs."

"It was your idea," Sid said, pointing his glass at me.

"I never thought you would do it," said Godfry.

"Completely ruthless," said Harlen, "Coach Bogart was fuming. We had a good chance to pick up a medal in that race."

"You guys are taking the piss. I don't remember any of this. Did Coach Bogart know we got disqualified on purpose?"

I had always respected the Coach's crotchety devotion, shaded optimism.

"I never told him."

"I doubt it."

"I think I would've remembered his reaction. If he'd known, he'd've killed you."

"How much money did you all give me? I asked, still not believing."

"Five bucks each," Brent said.

"I threw a race for fifteen bucks?"

"You were a kid. Fifteen bucks was a lot back then."

"Selective memory. Dude, you did it."

"Pure mercenary. Ice cold man."

The fire crackled. A spark flew onto the carpet. I stood up and extinguished the glint with my father's borrowed work boot. I felt like saying something angry but didn't.

"I'm going to drain the weasel."

Instead of going down the stair to the men's dressing room, I went out the back door and looked over the course from the teeing ground ledge. Flakes flurried and spun, moon reflecting off the vast white. Ski and snowmobile and deer tracks could be followed. I undid my pants and watched the snow dribble yellow. The air was cold on my skin. A cold I had forgotten since moving to Columbia. As I was zipping up, I heard a voice:

"So this customer says to me, 'I got a tip for you. Don't eat yellow snow!'"

I hear Wally's laugh morph into a cough. I turn

to see a cigarette dangling from a smile.

"Jeez ,Wally don't scare me like that."

"Afraid you gonna fall off the ledge and toboggan down with your willy out?"

"Some things never change."

We shared some silence. He offered me a smoke.

"You ever miss this place?" Wally asked me.

"Sure, all the time. It's a good place. A beautiful place."

"Then why did you leave?"

"Just to see what other places are like, I guess. Just to see."

"If you don't leave home, you ain't got no home to come home to, right?"

"Something like that, Wally. Something like that."

"Well, I better get back in there and stoke the fire. You guys want another round?"

"Sure, set one up. Hey, Wally. Can I ask you something?"

"Sure, but I don't know if I got any answers."

"You know me pretty well. Huh? I mean we were neighbors and classmates for what twelve, fifteen years? You know me, right?"

"Yeah I know you."

"Would you say I was ruthless?"

Wally threw his cigarette butt into the white snow. He looked at me then rubbed his hands together and blew on them to keep them warm.

"Ruthless, naw, but an opportunist? For sure."

"What do you mean? "

"You do what you say you will and you get what you want."

"I'll take that as a compliment, Walt."

"Take it any way you can get it, but my ass is freezing. Back to the grindstone. Hasta luego, hermano."

He swung the glass door open and began stamping his boots to get the snow off. I watched him go behind the bar. A carload of overly-made up high school girls came in the front door. I watched Wally crack a joke through the glass window and could hear their laughter. He started taking their orders.

I went back to the fire and my old friends, finally realizing why I never enjoyed team sports.

ROBERT VANDER LUGT

If I Had a Hammer

Every Sunday Ray watches the cars parade into East Presbyterian's parking lot. Usually he sits on the small, screened porch, coffee propped on his knee. On hot mornings, like this one, Ray wears a threadbare T-shirt and grey boxers. He assures Grace no one can see him through the screen. She smiles and shakes her head.

He knows the cars, their order of arrival. The old folks come first, parking near the doors and gripping the iron railing as they navigate the steps. The young families pull in next, assembling car seats and diaper bags, herding toddlers through the door. Then Grace walks out on the porch and stops beside him. Often she brings him breakfast—toast topped with a shiny egg. Sometimes she just stands quietly until he turns. "I'm going now," she says. She holds her small black purse tight against her trim waist. She still looks so good, Ray thinks. "Wish you'd come," she says. Ray nods and smiles. She leans to kiss him.

"Maybe next week." Ray receives her kiss. He runs his big hand lightly around her back. "I'll make dinner." He watches her push the screen door open, descend the steps, and cross the street. She stops outside the heavy arched doors of the church and turns. He knows she can't see him, but she waves anyway. Then she swings the big door open and disappears.

When they first moved here, thirty-four years ago, Ray went too, slipping into the back pew, standing and singing and always following Grace's lead. He shook hands and endured introductions, waiting while she made conversation, learning those strange people with their flat vowels and stern faces. Back then, it was a church of carpenters and tradesmen. New in town and out of work, Ray hedged about his past, unsure of their view of the long and now ended war. Most listened without judgment. Some offered suggestions about who might be hiring.

A few days later, the black rotary phone on the wall of their tiny kitchen rang. Grace handed the receiver to Ray and rested her hand soft on his shoulder. Ray listened, said yes two or three times, stood, and hung the phone back in place. "One of the old men from the church." he said. "Asked me to help fix up a house for some Vietnamese refugees." Grace nodded. "No pay, mind you. All volunteer." Grace smiled and left the room. "Now don't go getting your hopes all up," he called after her. After a few minutes, he went to the garage. He shuffled through stacks of unpacked boxes, until he found his carpenter belt.

Sawdust sifted from the empty nail pouches. The hammer still nested in its loop.

Ray worked alongside the men for two weeks. A big, balding carpenter with a fading Semper Fi tattoo on his forearm ran things, handing out assignments, checking work, scowling often. Ray watched the church folks, skilled and otherwise, patch walls and hang doors, scrub sinks and update wiring. Each night the house crowded with volunteers, so many that the hallways clogged like stopped drain pipes. Eager parents equipped their children with scrub brushes and brooms. Once Ray watched a mother slap her teenage son's face so hard, Ray winced. Just before, Ray heard the boy mutter something about cleaning a house for a bunch of gooks.

One evening the father of the refugee family toured the house. He was led around by the big carpenter and a translator, smiling and bowing, somehow standing proud among all those towering Dutch folk. Ray retreated to the backyard. Shaking, he lit a cigarette and squatted, squinting at the house. His right hand formed a fist. He forced it open and pressed it flat against his leg.

Over the next six years, three families occupied the house, found jobs, learned halting but sufficient English, and moved on. They politely attended services with their sponsors and then slowly returned to their own religious affiliations. They were Catholics and Buddhists and unbelievers. Ray found permanent work with the big carpenter. A refugee himself, Ray hung at the edges of the church. Then, like the smiling people with their strange customs, he quietly drifted away.

Ray waits until he hears music carry from the church. He listens, then rises and carries his cup to the kitchen. He tugs on a pair of battered jeans and strolls through the porch and down the steps. The Sunday paper lays rolled in its plastic skin. He peels it free and sits. The front page is cluttered with war and rumors of more. Promises of troop withdrawal. Warnings of new conflict. He snorts, shaking his head at the U.N.'s strongly worded warning to Syria. Locally, the city police declare war on street gangs. Ray ignores the rest, then tosses it through the screen door. The music from the church stops and Ray imagines the preacher reading the scripture before the sermon. Above, the sun nears its peak in the steel blue sky. He begins to walk.

Two blocks from their house, a two-story building stands surrounded by scaffolding. Ray stops to watch a crew of volunteers, dark-haired men, some bearded, scrabbling up ladders, mix mortar, pass concrete blocks from gloved hand to gloved hand. Cars crowd the dusty lot. There is not a pick up truck in sight.

Ray had marked their progress for months. The building sat quiet for weeks at a time, then burst upward in spasms. A painted plywood sign displays the finished building. Its strange characters are probably Arabic, but to Ray they may as well be Vietnamese. Grace has often mentioned the church's puzzlement over this new neighbor. They've held prayer meetings and invited experts on Islam to speak. Finally, Grace and a few others formed a welcoming delegation. "Well?" Ray asked when she returned, "Did you build any bridges?" Grace shrugged. "Build?" She said, "No, but maybe we chipped away at some walls."

A group of men assembles around a bunk of two-by-fours. They begin carrying stacks of lumber through the arched opening that will be the front door. Ray listens as a saw whines, the familiar clatter of cut offs hitting the floor. Then the competent rhythm of hammer blows. They're doing all right, Ray thinks. He stands in the shade of a big maple and watches, patting his pockets for a phantom pack of cigarettes. He quit years ago, but the memory lingers.

Ray crosses the street and wanders back. When the first tower came down, he was at work, arguing with a plumber about the clumsy holes he'd just drilled through a joist. The news from New York trickled from the painter's radio, but they were too busy to understand. Who could make sense of planes crashing into skyscrapers anyway? But as the enormity descended, they all gathered around the paint-splattered radio and listened, cursing softly, glancing at the sky. Some broke the circle, sat in their trucks and called their wives. Finally, Ray sent everyone home.

Ray stops just short of the church. The last time he went inside, except to complete some repair Grace volunteered him for, was the night of September 11. People arrived throughout the afternoon, bewildered, in need of each other. The pastor opened the doors, and by 7:00 p.m. a packed church gathered for prayer. Ray walked beside Grace through those big, sun-grayed doors and stood with head bowed. Grace wept. The pastor prayed mercy on an unknown enemy and comfort for all. Grace reminded him of that later, when the nation roiled for vengeance and the machines of war clattered.

The music begins again, a triumphant hymn sending them out. Ray crosses the street, angling toward the house. Inside, he fixes a light lunch, eats his portion and leaves Grace's in the fridge. Then he laces his work boots.

When Grace steps outside, she sees Ray—car-

penter's bag slung from his shoulder, hammer swing-
ing—walking toward the mosque.

TARA T. BOYCE

On Behalf of Love

I fell in love for the first time in eighth grade with a blond-haired blue-eyed boy who was seven months younger than me. We had social studies, P.E., and science together.

I remember now those last few months of the school year. The second the last period bell rang and Mark and I had to say goodbye to each other after P.E. class, I fell into a moody depression, in which I would return home to my room, turn on my CD player and listen to Beach Boys' "Don't Worry Baby" over and over, lying on my bed, staring at my purple ceiling, sometimes tearing up with heart-yearning. This happened most evenings, until I woke up way too early the next morning, put on my stereo again, and took thirty minutes to bathe (I always bathed because it was much more romantic). I would then blow dry and curl my hair, and apply the little makeup I was allowed to wear.

I remember the last day of my eighth grade year. It was bright, it was June, and the sun had this daring power over me. Mark had just signed my yearbook, "Your future's so bright, I've gotta wear shades," which made me laugh and love him even more as we walked together to his bus. This would be the last time I would see him for a long time, and I felt nauseous, as if someone opposed to my loving Mark had tightened a fist around my stomach. Still, I laughed all the way to his bus because in moments like these, all you want to see is the sun shining in the middle of the open sky, the bus still so many feet away, and the way you both shine together in the sun, listening to each other's pauses.

We took our time and let the others get on the bus before him until we could stall no longer. As he walked up the steps onto the bus, my heart bounced wildly—hearts really do bounce and jump and wobble—and I cried out, "Wait! I have to tell you something." He stopped and looked at me and I ran up the steps to him. "I have to tell you something," I said, although I didn't know what it was I had to say.

"A secret," I said. He smiled and leaned in and I, I laughed that nervous, Is this real? laugh I always laugh when something enormous is about to happen. I cupped my hand over my mouth and leaned into his ear and kissed his cheek. Then I ran away.

My legs and my lungs cheered as I ran because I had finally shown Mark Speck that even though I was seven months older than him, even though I was Mormon and he was Catholic, even though I was going away to high school and he was staying behind, I still, I still, loved him and oh, how it felt to prove it.

§

I am still learning more about love as I grow older—how it changes shape and color the older it gets. Though I still take baths because warm, soapy water will always be romantic, kisses on the cheek are no longer a secret, and I no longer feel the need to run from them—I married Ryan because I no longer wanted to. I also no longer feel like puking when Ryan is away. Instead, I want him to come back and I believe he will and I believe that is worth celebrating.

And yet sometimes I wonder what would happen to my understanding of love if he never came back. Or if we both, someday, wanted to leave, like my grandparents or my friends' parents or my own parents. I am tempted—with all the statistics in the world to back me up—to say love fades in and out like a rainbow trout in between shadow and sunwater. We keep reaching at it because—well, because it's just so mysteriously beautiful. If only we could hold it and keep it and that brilliant wet sheen could last forever.

Perhaps I disgrace love by suggesting this: that

love could ever fade. Perhaps it is we who fade, and our mortal inability to experience anything without growing tired of it makes us most unworthy of love. Perhaps love is not the fish in this metaphor. We are. Are we not transformed as if through water and light when we experience such a thing as love?

§

I'm remembering a year ago, when everyone from the congregation was invited to share at the pulpit. A woman walked up to the microphone and faced us. She said she had had a hard month, but she just had to come up, even if it meant leaving her three little red heads wrestling in the bench. She told us she loved her husband, who was sitting near the pulpit behind her, and that she didn't know how he did all he did, but she loved him for it.

I saw the way her husband looked at her, as shy and quiet as he is. He had to look up because he was sitting and she was standing. I saw the way his face flushed the color of his hair—he had given all her children their red hair—not with embarrassment, but with what looked like a sort of desperation be-cause how could he ever do any of it without her?

As she finished, her husband stood up too soon, before she finished saying amen. He hugged her there, beside the pulpit. He hugged her for a long time, in front of all of us, and those of us who were watching, we hushed ourselves and reverenced ourselves because we knew we were not just witnessing, but partaking something of the sacred.

§

More than the big extraordinary moments—the first kiss on the cheek, the first date, and someday, the first child—I see love in those small moments that happen not just once but again and again and again, whether or not anyone is looking at us.

§

This month we celebrated Valentine's Day. Rumor has it we celebrate this day because of an old Saint who, they say, secretly performed marriages for young soldiers unable to marry—marriage, that evil distraction, was outlawed for those poor Roman soldiers. They say Valentine was sent to prison for his secret ceremonies, and that he sent the first "valentine" to the daughter of his jailer who would visit him in his cell. "From your Valentine," he wrote her, just before they sentenced him to death.

To me the most romantic part is that the girl visited him. Over and over.

The truth is we don't know if Saint Valentine existed, what he did, or why we celebrate him with so many flowers and balloons and chocolates. Still, every year I find myself choosing to believe the rumors, not because I want to get presents or because I love any reason to celebrate (which I do), but because I believe in celebrating what we are each made from and what I believe we are each made for.

I think again of the girl who visited Valentine, perhaps early in the morning when he was feeling most alone. Perhaps he saw her not through rose-tinted glasses, but through iron bars. I imagine her kneeling across the dusty, stone floor, whispering that no matter what happened to him God knew him, she knew him, and he was made to be remembered. And I am thinking now, aren't we all?

I wonder if love taught Valentine and the jailer's daughter that purpose can be glimpsed even in the darkest of places. I wonder if they glimpsed this in each other as they looked through those bars. And I wonder now if love exists entirely separate from us. If so, how insignificant and powerful we are.

§

The other night I dreamt of rain, which fell all over the wooden back porch of the first home I remember living in. There were many of us there and we all wore my favorite colors—yellows, reds, oranges.

There were bright blue buckets all over the porch, all around us, filling up with rain. And when the buckets started to overflow, to burst over, we all laughed. Then, we got on our backs.

We opened our mouths to the sky. We lay there on our backs for a long time, drinking and drinking, filling until we were full and then full again.

When I awoke from the dream, I leaned over in the dark and reached for my notebook (I didn't want to wake Ryan). I wrote down what I could remember of that small moment of candescence, of what it felt like to lie there, face-up and open.

I rolled over and hugged Ryan, then rolled back onto my back. I stared at the black ceiling for a few minutes, thinking.

Not why, not when, but how: to ever fill, to ever be filled, to ever drink in, to ever quench?

DEB ATWOOD

Baby Carrot

They arrived at seven. The door opened and Logan, blond, assured, highball glass in hand, brought them inside. Evelyn glanced at Parker whose amber-colored face had already assumed a distant look.

Logan led Parker away, leaving Evelyn and Kendra to wander into the living room where Evelyn's mother-in-law Judith found them. Her hair was still red, Evelyn noted. Subtle. Expensive.

The room had not changed much since Evelyn's only other visit years ago, timeless in the way taste had always presumed to be. A worn Persian rug in umber and burgundy blended with the dark oak floor. To the side stood an ebony baby grand piano, but Evelyn's eye was drawn to the tall mullioned windows where drapes pooled in oyster-white waterfalls.

Kendra walked to the window seat. "Mom, look," she said.

Evelyn moved to Kendra's side. A porcelain nativity scene sat on a rosewood platform.

The glazed donkeys of muted browns, Mary's robe in robin egg blue—all were outlined with a delicate sheen.

"It's so beautiful." Kendra bent to admire the crèche while Evelyn combed her fingers through Kendra's glossy hair.

"I see you've found my joy." Judith had come up behind them. She reached in and brought out the Baby Jesus, wrapped in a square of flannel, from its bed of straw in the manger.

Or was manger the right word? Evelyn remembered the phrase "lay in a manger" but was that the straw trough or the stable itself? Damn this word befuddlement that lurched in and out. Perhaps her estrogen needed adjusting. Again.

"I love this set," Judith said. "Logan brought it from Europe time before last." She smiled. "My perfect son."

And where, Evelyn wondered, did that leave Parker? Imperfect son?

Evelyn studied the manger as Judith replaced the figurine, remembering now manger was the trough. So Logan had brought it from Europe time-before-last. Time-before-last, ha! The only time Parker had visited Europe was when Judith banished him to boarding school in Edinburgh.

Judith laid a hand on her arm and said, "How are you feeling, Evelyn. Really?"

Yes, Judith charmed people—the warm gaze, the

friendly grasp. Evelyn tried not to draw away. "Some days are better than others."

Judith's fingers massaged Evelyn's wrist. "I had that same surgery, you know."

"What?"

A hysterectomy? Judith?

"Parker didn't tell me," Evelyn murmured.

"Oh, it was years ago. Shortly before Parker came to us."

Interesting. Evelyn glanced at Parker who inclined his head to listen to his brother Logan. She fingered her locket.

After dinner, Logan suggested a game of I Spy. To choose turns, his wife Marta set an empty champagne bottle on the table and gave it a spin. Suddenly warm, Evelyn shifted, loosened her collar and freed her locket where it had caught on a button.

"Mom, you're first," Kendra said.

Evelyn looked at the table. The motionless bottle pointed at her across from the centerpiece, a large glass epergne.

"Something beginning with E," Evelyn said.

"You have to say 'I spy with my little eye,'" Kendra whispered, so Evelyn did.

The guests tried different objects. Marta even ventured, "It's Evelyn, right?" but no one guessed.

"No, it's the epergne," Evelyn said.

Their brows furrowed in disapproval as if she dared to out-culture them with a French word they did not know.

She considered the centerpiece that had caused the discord. Between candle flutes, crystal bowls held silver foil chocolates, and red and white roses carved from radishes and florets of cauliflower, all scalloped with tiny lettuces and edged with baby carrots. Perfect miniature, edible vegetables dressed as art, washed with egg white to glisten in candlelight. For the price of these tiny vegetables, probably never to be eaten (she pictured the maid Inga dumping them down the disposal), she imagined one could buy proper large vegetables and supply an orphanage in Shanghai.

Picking up a baby carrot, Evelyn rolled it with her fingers and cradled it in her palm.

Was it hot in here?

"I said…" Marta was talking to her, resting a hand on Evelyn's shoulder. "The epergne was very clever."

But it seemed to Evelyn that Marta's eyes held a challenge.

Marta spun the bottle, unsurprised when it pointed at her. "I spy with my little eye something beginning with L." Marta scrutinized Evelyn's throat.

"I know," Judith exclaimed, following Marta's gaze. "Locket."

"May I?" Marta asked. "I've been admiring it all evening." Eyebrows lifted, she reached over to trace the engraving. When her thumb prodded the edge, the locket popped open. "Oops."

Evelyn gasped.

"Sorry," Marta said. "I see Kendra, so cute! And who's this?"

The open locket framed two pictures. Evelyn had loved the locket because it didn't open all the way flat. The pictures remained close like sisters. In one, Kendra wore her favorite green dress. Facing her was Meifing.

Meifing's hair was darker than Kendra's, hanging straight, hooked behind her ear. She was two years old in the photo, solemn, staring into the camera. The locket's vintage glass glazed the pictures with a delicate sheen.

Parker's mouth opened. His face paled. Of course, he didn't know she still carried Meifing's picture.

Naturally, Evelyn had made a copy—yes, Meifing would always belong to her—before returning Meifing's referral photos and case study to the adoption agency.

That was after Evelyn had tried to reason with Parker.

"Don't you see," she said. "It's too late to change your mind. For me, it's too late. Let me call the agency back." When he didn't answer, she said, "Look at her picture, damn it!" And she stuck Meifing's photo under his nose. He'd walked away. Now, tonight, Parker was forced, finally, to face the photo in front of people who had made his own adoption a nightmare.

Tears standing in her eyes, Evelyn gave Parker the slightest of nods, a message. Yes, I see how it was for you here. But it wouldn't have been like that for us, for you and me and Kendra and Meifing.

Parker's eyes narrowed. He turned his head, leaving her to answer the guests: Who is that other girl?

Judith put down her champagne glass. "Evelyn, do tell."

Evelyn stiffened, her breath caught. The fingers that curled around the baby carrot dug into her flesh, and sweat dampened the starched white napkin until the poinsettia embroidered in scarlet began to bleed. She should never have worn wool, should have known the house would be overheated, that even one glass of wine—and it might have been more— could upset her.

Stomach churning, Evelyn mumbled, "Excuse me," to no one in particular.

Judith sat forward. "Evelyn? Dear?"

She must have air. Bolting from the room, Evelyn passed the sofa table holding the silver frames, averted her eyes, tried not to look at the picture of Marta and Logan in San Francisco when they had not bothered to call, reached the door, supported herself with the handle and cracked it open. She closed her eyes.

Behind her Judith said, "Inga, serve the mousse now, please."

Turning her sweat-drenched back to the cold air, Evelyn opened her eyes. That was when she spied the nativity scene. She closed the door and crossed the living room and stood in front of it. After a moment, she reached in and removed the baby figurine. With the square of flannel that had encircled the porcelain infant, she swaddled the baby carrot that was still in her palm and laid it in the manger.

LISA BURGESS

The Driver

Lila reached past the steering wheel and adjusted the volume on the radio. "A storm of at least twelve bombings ripped across Baghdad this morning, killing at least seventy-two people...." For years she had found the calm voices of the news reporters on NPR soothing after a long day. This day was no exception.

Without a word, her husband reached out and twisted the volume dial back down so that Lila had to strain to hear voices. "The developments heighten fears of a new round of Shiite-Sunni sectarian bloodshed...." She squinted through the glare of the streetlight as it reflected off her spectacles and could barely see where the yellow line separated the turn lane from the road. White gusts of snow swirled angrily across her windshield. Lila switched on her blinker and pulled into the turn lane.

Earlier that day, the perky girl-of-a-meteorologist on the television had been calling this a winter storm watch and warning people to stay inside if they could, if they had nowhere else they needed to be. Lila resented this warning. The girl appeared to be in her late thirties, young enough to be her daughter—if she had ever had one. And if she had, she would have taught her never to wear a bright red suit or tacky pink lipstick that poked out toward the camera every time she used the phrase, "Winter solstice." Apparently this meteorologist was keenly interested in the fact that tonight would be the longest night of the year.

It was dark out. A gap in the steady flow of headlights opened up ahead, and Lila turned left into the parking lot of the diner. "A suicide bomber driving an explosives-laden vehicle blew himself up outside the office of...." She pulled into a parking space and turned the key, killing the engine. The calming voice of the reporter cut off immediately. A cold, dark silence ensued. She waited for the inevitable crabby announcement from the passenger's seat: One, two, three—"Oh, hell. Let's just order at the drive-thru."

Right on cue, she thought, turning the key toward the dashboard and allowing the engine to cough, inhale, sputter, and then groan back to life, resurrecting the voices from NPR along with it: "After the guards let the ambulance driver through, he drove to the building where he blew himself up."

Shifting the car into drive, she pulled through the darkness surrounding the diner and pressed the brake when she came to the glowing, screen-like menu. "May I take your order?" a disembodied voice asked. She hated the drive-thru. She wanted to turn around, park, and go into the clean, well-lit diner. She wanted to demand they eat a meal at a table together, but the language between them had dissolved some time ago. She couldn't remember exactly when. Before his affair—she was sure of that. But how long before, she was never able to say. He'd told her he was sorry a hundred times, but his apologies sounded like a flute solo masked by the discordant bellows of a dozen bassoons. He'd offered to file for a divorce, if that was what she wanted, but she'd told him she wanted to work things out.

But really, she had no intentions of repairing their relationship.

Her true intentions? She guarded them, especially from herself, as if they were the face of Medusa. She knew if she looked at them she would surely turn to stone. And so she hid the fact that she really wanted to stay married because she enjoyed making him suffer. She wanted to transform herself into a scar, a burn—stretched pink skin, like raw, dried out meat, right across one cheek. A reminder of his misstep that he must look at every single day, for the rest of his life, and remember how beautiful he used to be. She wove a shroud of winter darkness, and it fell like a curtain between them.

And then, one day, something horrible happened: her stone-cold punishment stopped working. For a while—a year at least—he had been like an abused dog, cowering through the back door each evening after work, and hanging his coat neatly in the closet before taking a seat at the kitchen table. He would offer her submissive conversation speckled with sycophantic praise—to which she always returned as ice, of course. But now, now he seemed to have established a certain level of immunity against her punishments. He'd been playing cards with the guys on Tuesdays, just like he did before the affair. The number of times he called her each day dwindled from five to one—and she felt the one would return to zero rather soon. So now what? She was nearing retirement, childless, unhappy in her career, and unhappy in her marriage. He called her bluff, and now she was going to have to file for divorce. But worse, her main source of enjoyment—tormenting her husband—would melt into a memory, and then slowly, she would evaporate.

He shouted his burger-and-fries order over her lap, and as she contemplated the value of a diet coke over a chocolate shake, she wondered, when this had become her life? A thoughtless, unexamined crawl toward, toward what? But, there was always a choice—wasn't there?—a well-lit diner even in the darkness of a winter solstice?

Her mind wandered backward through the news report....

"Do you want to get away for a while" she asked, eyebrows raised.

He looked up at her, surprised. "Where?"

"I don't know. Florida maybe? Or Vegas?"

He shrugged. "I don't know if we can afford it right now."

Why had she ordered a salad? She didn't really like salads. In the past she had eaten them to keep her weight down, to keep herself healthy. But now, neither of those mattered. She did it out of habit, she supposed, pulling forward to the pickup window where she accepted her dinner.

Outside the streetlights stood like executioners uniformed in holly, red ribbon and masked in snow. She exited the parking lot and slowed the car to a stop behind a line of about fifteen other cars waiting for the light to turn green. The sound of a siren and red, flashing lights in her rearview mirror forced her to inch to the side of the road. Waiting, she was always waiting.

It was at this moment that she realized her hands were shaking. I'm cold, she explained to herself, it's so cold outside, so dark, the darkest day of the year, and then a thought appeared to her like a prophecy and a shiver of delight slid down her spine and the thought glowed on her dashboard and it shimmered and it looked through her and the sensation was like nothing she'd felt in years, like she had been sinking down through the darkness of the ocean, and now she was swimming up up up and breathe! "You're listening to NPR news. It's 5:30."

The streetlights melted into cowering mounds of holly and ribbon. A smile crawled up through her esophagus, into her throat and then pulled at one cheek. Her trembling hands turned the wheel to the left and her foot made its way to the gas pedal. "Lil? What are you—" The siren roared. And then a crash, glass shattering, metal bending, a scream.

The thought had become flesh.

When the second ambulance arrived just minutes later, both the old man and the woman were proclaimed dead upon impact.

"Long night?" the police officer politely asked the EMT.

The EMT lifted the first covered gurney into the falling snow. "The longest."

About the Authors

Marla Cantrell lives and writes in Arkansas. She is the managing editor of @Urban Magazine (aturbanmagazine.com). Most of Marla's stories deal with the South, the characters who populate it and the ties they have to the land they love.

Patricia W. Hunter is a freelance writer, a blogger at Pollywog Creek (pollywogcreek.com), and a photographer. She lives outside of Fort Meyers, Florida. You can follow Patricia on Twitter (@PatriciaWHunter).

Nancy Vandre lives in North Carolina with her husband and son. She has been journaling unprofessionally since she was six.

Dominic Laing grew up in San Jose, California and currently lives, works and writes as a member of Neighborhood Film Company, a Philadelphia-based production company that employs and mentors adults recovering from various cycles of addiction, poverty, and homelessness. He blogs at dominclaing.com. You can follow him on Twitter (@dominic_laing).

Kristi Boyce is fluent in Arabic and is a resident of Salt Lake City. She blogs at The Lady Doth Protest Too Much (kristiandbrock.blogspot.com). You can also find her on Twitter (@kristiboyce).

Morgan O'Connor grew up in a small village on Lake Huron. He has lived in New York, London, Sao Paulo, Toronto, Dublin, Doha, Nice, Sevilla, Verona, Miami, Barcelona, and his current home, Rio de Janeiro. He taught English at The University Of Miami and Universitat Autónoma de Barcelona and spent fifteen years working as a professional actor. He is currently at work on his first novel.

Robert Vander Lugt lives in Grand Rapids, Michigan with his wife and their children. He helps run a family business and is currently pursuing a writing degree from Calvin College. He blogs at seekingsomeday.blogspot.com.

Tara T. Boyce is a graduate student in English and a writing instructor at Brigham Young University in Provo, Utah. She is currently studying how aesthetic works are rhetorical, particularly how narrative forms work within us. Outside of reading Kenneth Burke and grading "research" papers, she spends her spare time admiring or making fun of her husband, writing about deep ideas on her blog (except for the not-so-deep ideas, like eating Cheetos), occasionally watching BBC series in the bathtub, and always, always wishing she was more productive with her time. After she graduates, she promises she'll do something worthwhile, like have a bunch of kids, write a book, save a life, etc. You can read more of her writing on her blog (taraboyce.wordpress.com).

Deb Atwood earned her MFA from Saint Mary's college in the Bay Area of California where she lives. Her novel *Moonlight Dancer* was published this year. She can be found on her blog, Pen in Her Hand (peninherhand.wordpress.com), and on Twitter (@deb_atwood).

Lisa Burgess is a high school English teacher, a writer, and a mom. She lives in Michigan and is particularly inspired by the short stories of Flannery O'Connor.

www.ingramcontent.com/pod-product-compliance
Lightning Source LLC
Chambersburg PA
CBHW020808130626
46554CB00006B/2339